Cleonardo

The Little Inventor

WRITTEN AND ILLUSTRATED BY

Mary GrandPré

ARTHUR A. LEVINE BOOKS · AN IMPRINT OF SCHOLASTIC INC.

Magellanardo

Sapphonardo

Leonardo

Neandernardo

Geonardo's workshop was built on top of his house, which was built on top of a hill at the foot of the mountains. Like his parents and grandparents and great-greats before him, Geonardo was an inventor. He hammered and welded metals of all kinds to build his big inventions for the little town where he lived with his father, Leonardo, and his daughter, Cleonardo Wren.

Cleonardo Wren wanted to be an inventor too, and she had great ideas.

"How 'bout some sticky bug vine, Dad?" she suggested one day, holding out a perfect specimen for him.

"Oh, I don't think so, little bird," he chuckled, tightening a bolt.

The town's annual Grand Festival of Inventions was coming up, and Cleo Wren was determined to help her father with his project.

"This is perfect!" she said.

"Er, that's a bit slimy, little bird," he replied.

Cleo Wren came back a few minutes later.
"How about THIS!" she shouted.

"How about passing me a wrench," her father
said with a small smile. "Now step out of the way.
I don't want you to get hurt."

So Cleo Wren decided to make something of her own for the festival. The forest was full of treasures, from golden goo bamboo and tacky termite twine to poofy cloud feathers and glitter-winged butterflies.

With Grandpa Leo's help, she cleaned off a large fallen tree for her worktable. Her grandpa then gave her one of his favorite tools: a twisty, wooden-handled awl.

Finally, Cleo Wren held a wondrous creation in her hands: a tiny whirligig. It had a fine propeller made of fallen dragonfly wings. She pulled the tangled stem to see what would happen. . . . Would it fly?

The whirligig danced and spun in the air, until it bounced off a branch and back onto her worktable, sputtering and unharmed.

Cleo Wren couldn't wait to show her father.

"Oh, what a sweet little toy!" Grandpa exclaimed.

Sweet? Toy? Cleo Wren thought her father's inventions were BIG! IMPORTANT! She would have to do better.

"Your father will be over the moon when he sees this!" her grandpa went on.

"The moon!" Cleo Wren cheered. "That's it!"

She tucked the tiny whirligig into her shirt pocket and reached for a stick to sketch her idea. . . .

Back home, Geonardo sat at his worktable, missing his sweet daughter by his side. Without his little bird, the festival didn't seem very important.

Suddenly, he jumped up. "That's it! A BIRD! A flying mechanical bird! My little Wren will love it as much as the judges, and THEN she'll come back to my workshop!"

For three days and nights, daughter and father
worked on their soon-to-be prize-winning inventions.

She twisted, twirled, perched, and puffed.

He hammered, honed, wired, and welded.

Finally, the day of the contest arrived, and
Geonardo stood back, admiring his invention.
"Ahhh! Delicate and strong . . . just like my
Cleonardo Wren," he said proudly. He packed
the mechanical bird up carefully and then with
a joyful shout — "I'm off!" — headed to the
town square.

"Ahhh! Yes! Big and perfect . . . just like one of Dad's inventions," Cleo Wren whispered.

Grandpa helped her wrap the large, fluttering moon in a tablecloth.

"That's a lot to carry all the way to town, little one. Perhaps you should take my fishing boat," Leonardo offered.

Then, with her covered creation tied in securely, Cleo Wren paddled toward town.

Cleo Wren was amazed by all that she saw at the town square: inventions of every kind, on wheels, in cages, brightly painted, and elegantly gilded. Her stomach fluttered; would her moon even float? Was it good enough? Important enough? Big enough?

After a moment, the mayor began to call out names.

"First contestant," he bellowed, "GEONARDO!"

Geonardo stepped forward and lifted his mechanical bird high into the air, then gave it three good cranks.

"Fly, bird! FLY!" he cried.

The bird swooped and circled over the square with great precision. Cleo Wren beamed. There, on the belly of the bird, were golden letters spelling out her name.

But suddenly a gust of wind caught one wing and sent the metal bird wobbling off course! It began to swerve and spin out of control and seemed to be heading straight for the mayor himself!

"NO, BIRD! FLY! FLY!" called Geonardo.

Everyone seemed frozen in fear.

Everyone but Cleo Wren.

Instinctively she unleashed her invention out into the cool mountain breezes. If only she could get it between the bird and the mayor!

The moon floated upward, slowly but steadily. . . .

Ah! Finally! It blocked the bird on its first wobbly flight toward the mayor. But Cleo Wren's moon wasn't meant for zipping and zooming. The butterflies held it up gently in the air, floating in place. And her father's bird was still swooping around, heading once more for a crash that might hurt someone.

Cleo Wren clutched her hand to her heart and
there she felt something . . .

. . . the tiny whirligig.

Without a second thought, she wound it as fast and as tight as she could. She took careful aim, and . . .

Up, up, up it zoomed, like a spiky-tailed armored beetle.

In a split second, the tiny whirligig snagged the hollow reed-and-twig moon and carried it directly up to the damaged bird.

CRRRRRUNCH!!!!!

The bird was finally caged! With great strength, the tiny buzzing whirligig carried the broken pair over trees and past mountaintops until it was safely out of sight.

The contest resumed, and a small boy with a musical fountain won the prize.

"Sorry about your bird, Dad," said Cleo Wren.

"Sorry about your moon! And that WHIRLIGIG!" her father replied. "That was AMAZING! Want to show me how you did it?"

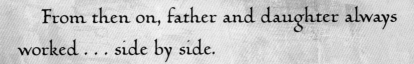

From then on, father and daughter always
worked . . . side by side.

Like Geonardo, my father was an inventor. He was also a carpenter
and a tinkerer. Spending time with him in his workshop opened the
door for me to explore and find my own way to create. I will always
be grateful for his adventurous and generous spirit. — M. G.

For my father,
always by my side.

LIBRARY OF CONGRESS CATALOGING-IN-PUBLICATION DATA
Names: GrandPré, Mary, author, illustrator.
Title: Cleonardo, the little inventor / written and illustrated by Mary GrandPré.
Description: First edition. | New York : Arthur A. Levine Books, an imprint of Scholastic Inc., 2016. | Summary: With the
town's annual Grand Festival of Inventions coming up, Cleonardo is determined to invent something impressive to enter,
something that will impress her inventor father Geonardo.
Identifiers: LCCN 2015043457 | ISBN 9780439357647 (hardcover : alk. paper)
Subjects: LCSH: Inventions—Juvenile fiction. | Fathers and daughters—Juvenile fiction. | Contests—Juvenile fiction. |
Competition (Psychology)—Juvenile fiction. | CYAC: Inventions—Fiction. | Fathers and daughters—Fiction. | Contests—
Fiction. | Competition (Psychology)—Fiction.
Classification: LCC PZ7.1.G722 Cl 2016 | DDC [E]—dc23 LC record available at http://lccn.loc.gov/2015043457

10 9 8 7 6 5 4 3 2 1   16 17 18 19 20
Printed in Malaysia 108
First edition, September 2016

The display and text type was set in Linotype Humanistika Regular.
The art for this book was made with rice paper collage and acrylic paint and dyes on watercolor board.
Book design by Mary GrandPré and David Saylor. Borders and endpaper designs created by Tom Casmer.